When 10-year-old Ben Tennyson stumbles upon a mysterious alien device in the woods one summer, little does he realise that his life is set to change - forever.

As soon as the watch-like Omnitrix quite literally gets a grip on him, Ben discovers it gives him the ability to transform into 10 different alien super-beings, each one with awesome powers!

Using the Omnitrix to cause super-powered mischief turns out to be fun, but will Ben learn to use his might to fight for good?

READ ON AND FIND OUT . . .

EGMONT
We bring stories to life

Published in Great Britain 2009
by Egmont UK Limited
239 Kensington High Street, London W8 6SA

Ben 10 and all related characters and elements
are trademarks of and © Cartoon Network.
(s09)

Adapted from the animated series by
Barry Hutchison

1 3 5 7 9 10 8 6 4 2

A CIP catalogue record for this title is available from
the British Library

Printed and bound in Great Britain by the CPI Group

CHAPTER ONE

MEET BEN TENNYSON

In the dark depths of outer space, a small alien spaceship dodged and weaved through a meteor shower. It spun and twisted to avoid the energy blasts of a much larger battleship that followed close behind.

BLAM! The smaller ship was suddenly thrown sideways as one of the blasts slammed into it. A direct hit!

The ship opened fire with its own weapons and burned two deep holes in the side of the battleship.

On board the monstrous battleship, a black-and-red robot studied the flashing lights on the computer screen. The smooth metal walls of the ship shuddered as another energy blast exploded against the outside.

'Hull damage, twenty per cent,' said the robot in a mechanical voice. 'Weapon systems still operational.'

Behind the robot, a huge, hulking alien leaned forwards in his command chair and narrowed his red eyes. Although he was half hidden by shadow, it was possible to make out his slimy green skin, his bald head and the row of tentacles that stuck out from his chin like a

beard. His name was Vilgax, and he was very, very angry!

'I have come too far to be denied!' the evil alien growled. He bunched his hands into fists. 'The Omnitrix shall be mine and there is not a being in this galaxy that dares stand in my way!'

❉ ❉ ❉

Meanwhile, in a classroom many millions of miles away, a boy named Ben Tennyson was hard at work. He was focusing his full attention on the sheet of paper on his desk, folding it over and over again.

The folding was finished and his masterpiece was complete. After making sure no one was watching, Ben picked up his paper aeroplane and launched it across the classroom.

He watched it swoop over the desks. He watched it float past the open window. Finally, he watched it curve sharply and crash, nose first, against the back of his teacher's head!

By the time the teacher had turned round, Ben had snatched up a book. He hid behind it, pretending to be reading, until she turned her attention back to the blackboard. Phew! That was too close!

The rest of the lesson seemed to go on forever. It was the last day of school before the summer, and all Ben could think about were the holidays. He and his grandpa were off camping – just the two of them. It was going to be great!

Eventually, the end of the day drew near. Ben sat perched in his seat and watched the final few seconds tick away. Ten seconds until the bell. Five seconds. Four, three, two, one!

BRRRRRRRRRRRING! The moment the bell started to ring, Ben leaped from his seat and rushed for the door.

'Yesss!' he laughed. 'I'm outta here!'

'Benjamin?' said the teacher sternly.

'Could I have a word with you before you go?'

Ben stopped mid-run and turned round. He swallowed hard when he saw the teacher was holding his paper aeroplane.

'Uh-oh,' he gulped. 'Busted.'

❈ ❈ ❈

A few minutes later, with his telling off still ringing in his ears, Ben finally escaped from school. He strolled through the playground, enjoying the sunshine, but enjoying his freedom even more. School was over. The holidays were just beginning. Good times lay ahead!

Ben turned a corner and spotted two older kids pushing a much smaller boy around. Ben recognised the younger boy as Jamie from his class. The bullies laughed as they shoved him hard against a tree.

'Normally we'd take your money and beat you up, but since it's the last day of school we're gonna give you a break,' snarled one of the bullies. He held out a dirty hand. 'Now hand over the cash!'

Jamie quickly reached into his school bag. If it meant he wouldn't get beaten up, he was happy to hand over any money he had.

'Leave him alone!'

The bullies spun round to find Ben standing nearby. They laughed when they saw him. Not only were they bigger than he was, but there were two of them and only one of him.

'Get lost, shrimp!'

'I said,' growled Ben, 'back off!'

'Looks like we got us a hero,' said the other bully. Both of them advanced menacingly. 'Suppose we don't want to back off?'

The bullies were almost upon Ben now. One of them leaned forwards as he spoke. 'What are you going to do about it, Tennyson?'

Ben narrowed his eyes and clenched his fists. It was time to teach these guys a lesson!

At least, that was the plan. Instead, Ben soon found himself dangling from a tree branch by his underwear. Jamie hung helplessly from the next branch over – another victim of the bullies' famous Atomic Wedgie!

'Thanks,' Jamie sighed. 'Thanks a lot!'

Shuddering, shaking and spitting out clouds of black smoke, a tatty motorhome stopped just outside the school gates. A friendly-looking old man wound down the window and leaned his grey-haired head out.

'Come on, Ben, let's go. We're burning daylight,' he shouted over. 'I want to make it to the campsite by nightfall.'

Ben rolled his eyes. 'Uh, Grandpa,' he called, 'a little help here?'

❋ ❋ ❋

Grandpa Max climbed back into the motorhome. The floor creaked and groaned as he made his way to the driver's seat. He didn't call the van The Rust Bucket for nothing!

Ben hopped inside, still adjusting his underwear. He pushed the door closed behind him and followed Grandpa.

'I've been so looking forward to this,' he grinned.

He stopped in his tracks as he realised they were not alone. His cousin, Gwen, was sitting at The Rust Bucket's dining table.

'What are *you* doing here?' he demanded. He spun back to face Grandpa Max. 'What is *she* doing here?'

'Take it easy, dweeb. This wasn't my idea,' Gwen explained. 'Somebody convinced my mom that going camping for the summer would be a good experience for me.'

'I can't *believe* it,' Ben moaned. 'I wait all school year to go on this trip and now the Queen of Cooties is along for the ride!'

'Hey, I had my own vacation already

planned out too, ya know,' replied Gwen. 'Now I'm stuck with my geekazoid cousin going camping for *three months*!'

'Geek,' Ben snapped.

'Jerk,' Gwen spat back.

Up at the front, Grandpa Max turned in his seat and started the engine. With a splutter, The Rust Bucket wheezed into life. As it pulled away from the school, Grandpa sighed quietly.

'Something tells me it's going to be a long summer.'

CHAPTER TWO

GOING HERO

Ben and Gwen sat at a picnic table, surrounded by hundreds of tall trees. They had arrived at the campsite just as the day was drawing to an end. It was dark now, with only their campfire to light up the night.

'Chow time!' Grandpa announced. He stepped down from The Rust Bucket holding a large plate. Ben sniffed the air. Dinner smelled fantastic! He hadn't realised until now how hungry he was.

But not *that* hungry. Ben stared down at the slimy mass on the plate Grandpa had set before them. Whatever it was, it looked disgusting. What was worse, it was moving!

'OK, I give up,' he said, watching helplessly as half his dinner began to crawl across the table. 'What *is* that?'

'Marinated mealworms,' announced Grandpa proudly. 'They're considered a delicacy in some countries.'

'And totally gross in others,' Gwen scowled.

'If these don't sound good, I've got some smoked sheep's tongue in the fridge.'

Neither option sounded appealing to Ben. 'Couldn't we just have a burger or something?'

'Nonsense!' laughed Grandpa. 'This summer is going to be an adventure for your tastebuds.' He turned and headed back towards the motorhome. 'I'll grab the tongue.'

'OK,' whispered Ben, leaning in close to his cousin, 'I got a half-eaten bag of corn chips and a candy bar in my back pack. What you got?'

'Some rice cakes and hard candy.'

Ben nodded. It wasn't much, but it was better than worms. 'Think we can make them last the whole summer?'

✳ ✳ ✳

In outer space, the two ships were still locked in battle. Their laser blasts were slower now, and it seemed the fight was almost over.

Vilgax's robotic second-in-command scanned the controls. 'Their propulsion systems have been destroyed,' it announced.

'Prepare to board,' barked Vilgax. 'I want the Omnitrix now!'

Before the robot could react, an energy blast exploded against the hull. Vilgax roared with rage as shards of glass and metal rained down on him.

Furious, he flipped open a panel on his chair. He managed to stab a clawed finger into the controls and activate the ship's most powerful weapon before another explosion hit the command deck.

A bolt of pure energy shot from the front of Vilgax's ship. It tore through the smaller ship as if it were made of paper. With a blinding flash, half of it was turned to specks of space dust.

Unseen by Vilgax, a hatch slid open in the belly of the shattered spacecraft. A small, round pod emerged and streaked off towards a distant blue-and-green planet.

The planet Earth!

Down on that very planet, Ben was walking in the forest near the campsite. He'd had enough of Gwen already, and needed some time by himself. Why did Grandpa have to bring her along? This was going to be the worst summer ever.

A movement overhead caught his eye. He looked up and saw a bright light streaking across the sky.

Ben stopped walking and watched the sparkling light. It seemed to be getting brighter. Brighter and bigger. Much, *much* bigger. At the last possible moment he realised the shooting star was shooting straight for him!

Ben threw himself out of the way just as the ground where he'd been standing exploded with a deafening ***BOOM!*** Large lumps of rock were thrown up into the air, and the whole area was covered by a choking cloud of dust.

When the smoke had cleared, Ben edged forwards. The meteorite had left a large, round crater in the middle of the forest. He crept closer and saw a small metal ball resting at the bottom of the hole.

Before he could figure out what the thing was, to his alarm the ground at Ben's feet crumbled. He slid down into the crater and skidded to a stop right next to the sphere. It hissed slightly as it opened, revealing an eerie green glow.

Ben leaned in closer. There was something inside the ball – something very un-alien.

'A watch?' he frowned. 'What's a watch doing in outer space?'

Without warning, the weird device leaped out of its protective shell. It wrapped round Ben's wrist and clamped on tight.

'Get it off! Get it off!' he shouted, frantically trying to shake the thing off his arm. He grabbed on to the black strap and heaved, but it wouldn't let go. The watch was stuck!

Ben pulled himself up out of the crater and staggered off in the direction of the

campsite. He yanked at the watch, still trying to take it off. No matter how hard he tried, though, it continued to cling on.

He studied the thing more closely. He couldn't see how he was supposed to tell the time with it. There were no hands on it at all. Instead, it displayed some strange symbols, with three green rings round the outside.

As he fiddled with the device, it suddenly let out a loud **BLEEP!** The middle of the watch raised slightly. Ben's eyes widened as a figure shaped like a man appeared on the display.

'Cool!'

He pushed the raised part of the watch back down. Instantly, a strange green energy swirled from it and snaked up his arm. As the energy passed across him, Ben felt his body begin to mutate.

First his arm bulged and grew, then his skin turned red and rough as rock. The changes quickly travelled over his shoulder,

up his neck and began to sweep across his face. He closed his eyes, terrified, as the transformation took hold.

When Ben opened his eyes, he was no longer quite himself. He looked down at his new body. He was adult sized and bright red from head to toe – however, something even stranger than that had happened: every single part of him was covered in flames! He didn't know it yet, but Ben had become an alien called Heatblast.

'I'm on fire! I'm on fire!' he cried, before he realised the flames weren't hurting him.

'Hey, I'm on fire and I'm OK!'

Heatblast glanced at a nearby tree. *Hmm*, he thought, *I wonder*.

He pointed to one of the lower branches. A blast of flame shot from his fingertip and blasted the wood to pieces.

'Now *that's* what I'm talking about!'

He squeezed his hands together. An orange flame flickered between them. It grew and grew until it became a swirling ball of fire.

The fireball shot from Heatblast's hands and ripped through a row of trees, snapping them in half. As the trees fell, the heat from the fireball ignited their leaves. They were still burning when they hit the ground.

'Wait! Stop!' yelped Heatblast, but it was too late. As the smouldering leaves hit the grass, the blaze quickly took hold. Within moments the damage was done.

The forest was on fire!

CHAPTER THREE

A FLAMING DISASTER

'What's that?' asked Gwen, pointing towards a bright glow in the sky above some nearby trees.

'Looks like the start of a forest fire,' Grandpa replied. 'We'd better let the ranger station know. Probably some darn fool camper out there messing around with something he shouldn't.'

Grandpa and Gwen stood in silence for a few moments, considering this. A terrible thought occurred to them both.

'Ben!'

'Better take this,' said Grandpa, throwing Gwen a fire extinguisher. After snatching up one for himself, they both set off in the direction of the glow.

* * *

In the heart of the forest, Heatblast was trying desperately to stamp out the fire. But every time his foot touched the ground, his flames set something else alight. This fire was getting well and truly out of control!

Even though the flames were close enough to burn him, Heatblast couldn't feel them. He should have been in agony, but the fire didn't hurt a bit.

'This would be cool if it weren't so *not* cool,' he mumbled to himself.

Suddenly, a blast of white foam hit him in the face. He coughed and spluttered, choking on the chemical spray. Blinded for a moment, he staggered and almost tripped.

When his eyes had cleared, Heatblast

found himself face to face with Gwen. Foam dripped from the nozzle of her fire extinguisher. She stared up at the alien for a few seconds, and then screamed at the top of her voice.

'I know I look weird,' Heatblast said, trying to calm her down, 'but there's no reason to be scared . . .'

But it wasn't Gwen who needed to be scared. Recovering quickly from her fright, she swung the heavy fire extinguisher with all her strength. It made a loud **CLANG** as it glanced off Heatblast's head. The force of the knock sent him tumbling to the forest floor.

Gwen raised the nozzle of the extinguisher and pointed it at the fallen alien. 'I don't know what you are, but you'll stay down there if you know what's good for you,' she warned.

Annoyed, Heatblast launched a few bolts of flame at Gwen's feet. She yelped with fright. One of her shoes had caught light! Hopping like mad, she blasted her foot with the fire extinguisher, then turned back to the alien. She held the extinguisher up, ready to deliver another crunching blow.

'I warned you!' she growled.

The alien's eyes narrowed. 'Don't even think about it, freak.'

That last word stopped Gwen in her tracks. 'Freak'. There was only one person who ever called her that.

'Ben?' she gasped. 'Is that you? What happened?!'

Taking a deep breath, Heatblast hurriedly filled her in on everything. He was just reaching the part where he'd accidentally set the forest on fire when Grandpa Max came running up.

'Gwen, are you all . . .' he began. He stopped when he spotted Heatblast. 'What in blazes?'

'Hey, Grandpa,' said Gwen, 'guess who?'

'It's me, Grandpa!'

'Ben?' frowned Grandpa. 'What happened to you?'

'Well, when I was walking, this meteor –'

'Um, excuse me,' Gwen interrupted, 'major forest fire burning out of control, remember?'

Heatblast and Grandpa looked around. The blaze now surrounded them.

'What do we do?'

Grandpa thought for a few moments. 'Backfire,' he said at last. 'Start a new fire and let it burn into the old fire. They'll snuff each other out.' He turned and looked at the blazing figure next to him. 'Think you can do that, Ben?'

'Shooting flames I can definitely do!'

He turned and ran straight for the nearest wall of flame. Without hesitating, Heatblast jumped through the fire. He kept running until he was standing in an untouched area of forest. Any second now the flames would reach these trees too. There was no time to lose.

Concentrating hard, Heatblast threw out his hands. He felt a hot surge of power build up inside him. It quickly shot along his arms. In a burst of blinding light, a jet of flame leaped from his fingertips.

The closest trees immediately caught alight, and it only took a few seconds for the new fire to take hold.

Heatblast turned off his flame-thrower fingers and watched anxiously. What if the plan didn't work? The blaze was spreading fast. What if, instead of solving the problem, he'd made things worse? He chewed his lip nervously. The plan had to work. It had to!

YESSS! Within minutes, the two fires met and began to snuff each other out. He'd done it! Heatblast had saved the day! With a little bit of help from his Grandpa, of course.

🕸 🕸 🕸

Vilgax was hurt, but he was alive. Just. He had lost more than half his body when the command deck had exploded. Now he floated in the yellow liquid of a Medi-Tube, breathing through the ship's life-support systems. His body would regrow, but it would take time.

'This battle nearly costs me my life,' he wheezed, 'and you say the Omnitrix is no longer on board the transport?'

His robotic second-in-command lowered

its polished head. 'Sensors indicate a probe was sent out from the ship just before boarding,' it explained. 'It landed on a nearby planet.'

What was left of Vilgax's face twisted into a scowl. 'Go,' he commanded. 'Bring it to me!'

�֎ ✖ ✖

Heatblast watched a marshmallow go brown in his hand. Within seconds it had dissolved into a squidgy goo. He popped it in his mouth. Mmm, tasty!

'And you say that this "watch" just jumped up and clamped on to your wrist?' asked Grandpa. They were sitting around the campfire and watching carefully to make sure nothing else went up in smoke.

'Hey, this time it wasn't my fault, I swear,' Heatblast insisted.

'I believe you, Ben,' nodded Grandpa.

'Think he's going to stay a monster

forever?' asked Gwen. Part of her secretly hoped the answer would be 'yes'.

'He's not a monster – he's an alien,' Grandpa replied. He realised Gwen and Heatblast were staring at him quizzically. 'I mean look at him,' he added quickly. 'What else could he be?'

'I don't want to be fire guy forever!'

'Don't worry, Ben, we'll figure this thing out.'

They all jumped with fright as the watch gave a loud **BLEEP!** Heatblast stood up as a few more beeps rang out. Just as the last one sounded, he was lit up by a bright, blinding flash.

Ben looked down at himself. His hands were his own. His clothes were his own. Even better, he was no longer on fire!

'I'm me again!' cried Ben. He gave the watch an experimental tug. 'But I still can't get this thing off.'

'Better not fool with it any more until we know exactly what we're dealing with,' warned Grandpa. He stood up and headed for the forest. 'I'll go check out the crash site. You guys stay here until I get back.'

Gwen and Ben watched him disappear into the trees. Neither of them noticed the sleek shape that sliced silently down from the sky above their heads.

CHAPTER FOUR

GIVE A DOG A DRONE

The robot stood at the edge of the crater, scanning for any sign of the Omnitrix. Its sensors soon detected the metal shell, but immediately realised it was empty. Someone had taken the watch! This was not good.

It raised a hand and unleashed a blast of energy. Instantly, the shell was reduced to a smoking pile of melted metal.

Two hidden compartments in the robot's shoulders unfolded, allowing a pair of spinning discs to fly free. They whizzed through the forest and, as they flew, a set of sharp metal claws extended below them both.

The robot watched them zoom off into the

trees. If the Omnitrix was nearby, they'd find it. It was only a matter of time.

❇ ❇ ❇

Ben sat with his back against The Rust Bucket, fiddling with the watch. He pressed, pushed, twisted and pulled, but he couldn't figure out what made the thing tick.

'Caught ya!' Gwen yelled. She burst out laughing when she saw how much she'd startled her cousin.

'Very funny,' Ben snapped. 'Like your face.'

'Grandpa said not to mess with that thing,' she reminded him.

'Come on,' said Ben, 'you can't tell me you aren't a little bit curious about what else this thing can do.'

'Not in the least.'

Ben looked her up and down. 'Are you

sure you're related to me?' He turned his attention back to the watch. 'Look, if I can figure this thing out, maybe I can help people. I mean really help them, not just, you know, make things worse.'

Despite herself, Gwen couldn't help but be curious. 'So what did it feel like,' she asked, 'going all alien like that?'

'It freaked me out at first,' replied Ben. 'It was like I was me, but also like I was somebody else.' He twisted the outside ring of the watch. With a **BLEEP!** the centre raised up once more. 'Hey, I think I've figured out how I did it,' he said. 'Should I try it again, just once?'

'I wouldn't.'

'No, duh,' Ben mocked, '*you* wouldn't.'

He slammed his hand down on the watch, and was immediately swallowed up by the cloud of weird energy. This time, though, there were no flames. Instead, Ben felt millions of thick, wiry hairs burst through his skin. Fangs as large as carving knives tore up through his bottom jaw, just as sharp claws sprouted from his fingers and toes. With an animal roar, Ben transformed into the savage Wildmutt!

'Eww!' Gwen winced. 'This thing's even uglier than you are normally. Bow wow, put a flea collar on this mutt.'

Wildmutt opened his mouth to reply, but all that came out were some strange grunts and groans.

'And no eyes?' scoffed Gwen. 'What good is this one? It can't see!'

A wicked thought suddenly occurred to her. Moving stealthily, Gwen picked up a stick and crept over to the huge, dog-like alien. She raised the stick like a cricket bat, then swung it, full speed, towards Wildmutt's butt.

The blind alien cocked his head. Its senses detected the threat, and powerful leg muscles sprang into action. Gwen gasped as the creature backflipped out of danger. The Rust

Bucket creaked and shook as Wildmutt landed on its roof.

'OK, so maybe it's not a total loser,' Gwen admitted. The alien leaped down from the motorhome and landed in front of her. She pulled away, covering her nose with her hands. 'Two words,' she choked, 'breath mints!'

Wildmutt snorted, then turned away. He kicked his back legs, spraying Gwen with mud and grass, before bounding off into the trees.

'Ben, get back here! Ben! I'm gonna tell Grandpa that you turned into some freaky animal-monster thing and went swinging around the forest when he told you not to.' She replayed her entire last sentence in her head. 'This,' she sighed, 'is a majorly weird day.'

✖ ✖ ✖

Wildmutt swung and leaped from branch to branch. He flipped and spun through the forest, easily jumping huge distances without any effort. Although he couldn't see, his other senses guided him. The whole area was alive with sounds and smells. They painted a picture for him; a picture of –

DANGER! He landed on a branch and paused. Something was terribly wrong. His thick, orange fur stood on end. Something bad was about to happen!

A laser blast lit up the woods and turned

the branch beneath Wildmutt to splinters. He leaped for another tree as one of the robot's deadly drones came spinning from the shadows.

With a grunt, the alien launched himself forwards. A sudden heat scorched his back and the tree he'd just swung from exploded in a shower of sparks. He gritted his sharp fangs. **FASTER** – he had to move faster!

Another tree erupted into flame. Wildmutt twisted to avoid the falling trunk. The stench of burning filled his nostrils. He could almost taste the smoke – thick, black and billowing. The perfect place to hide.

The drone slowed to a stop in a clearing and began scanning for any sign of the beast. Its sensors swept over the whole area, but found nothing. Something so large couldn't just vanish. Where could the alien be?

A sound from behind made it spin round. A snarling ball of orange fury sailed through the air, its curved claws outstretched. The flying

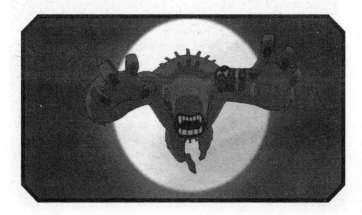

disc raised its weapons too late. Wildmutt
landed on it and immediately began to tear it
apart.

His teeth ripped into the drone's electrics.
It shot off through the trees, zigzagging left and
right, desperately trying to shake the beast off.
Wildmutt clung on with one paw and used the
other to claw through the disc's metal body. It
shook and shuddered beneath him. Time to get
off this ride!

Wildmutt jumped from the drone's back
and somersaulted to safety. The watch had
begun to bleep again, and as the spinning

disk exploded against the side of a large rock, the alien transformation wore off. He was Ben again.

'Yesss!' he cheered, spotting the shattered drone. He'd done it! He'd won!

A low humming sound caught Ben's attention. The second robot drone hovered down from the treetops, its weapons trained on him.

'Oh,' Ben gulped. 'Not good.'

CHAPTER FIVE

DIAMOND GEEZER

Ben tried to stumble away, but the drone hovered closer. It detected that the Earthling had the Omnitrix. It switched its weapon systems to full power. One blast would be enough to destroy the human.

It would take only three seconds for its guns to reach maximum strength. Three seconds. Two seconds. One sec –

CLANG! A spade smashed into the drone like an express train. The impact short-circuited its flight systems and it crashed on to the forest floor. It whirred round, scanning for whoever had attacked it. A red-haired girl stood over it, looking down.

'Back off, sparky,' Gwen snarled. She raised her spade and brought it down hard on the drone's robotic disc. 'No flying tree-trimmer is going to hurt my cousin.'

'I never thought I'd say this,' Ben smiled, 'but am I glad to see you!'

When Ben and Gwen were safely back inside The Rust Bucket, Grandpa began his lecture. Ben listened with his head hung low.

'I was worried that you might get popular with that thing on your wrist. That's why I asked you not to fool around with it until we know what the heck it is.'

'Sorry, Grandpa,' Ben said. 'But at least I figured out how to make it work.' He held up his wrist and pointed at the watch. 'All you do is press this button, then when the ring pops up just twist it until you see the guy you want to be. Slam it down and **BAMMO!** You're one of ten super-cool alien dudes!'

'What about staying a "super-cool alien dude" and not transforming back into plain old pizza-face?' Gwen scowled.

'I kinda haven't figured that part out yet,' admitted Ben.

Grandpa gave a sigh. This wasn't the camping trip he had expected.

'With a device as powerful as that watch clamped on you, my guess is we'd better help you learn fast,' he said.

With a loud crackle, The Rust Bucket's short-range radio unexpectedly hissed into life.

'Mayday! Mayday! Somebody help us!' pleaded a frightened voice. 'We're under attack by some sort of . . . I know you're not going to believe me, but *robot*!'

The rest of the transmission was drowned out by static, but it didn't matter. Ben had heard all he needed to hear.

'Sounds just like those things that attacked me,' he said as he stood up. 'It must be looking for the watch. Those people are in trouble because of me.' He took a deep breath and looked up at his grandfather. 'I think I can help them.'

'*You?*' Gwen scoffed. 'What are you gonna do about it, Tennyson?'

Ben threw open The Rust Bucket's door. Gwen and Grandpa followed him as he hurried outside. As he walked, he spun the outside ring of the watch.

'Eenie, meanie, minie . . .' He stopped at one of the alien outlines. 'Here it goes!'

BLEEP! went the watch. Ben's hand slammed down. A now familiar cloud of energy swirled across his body.

'So what can this guy do?' Gwen demanded, once the transformation was complete.

'I don't know.' Ben shrugged. He looked

down at his new body. It sparkled like a precious stone in the moonlight. 'But I bet it's gonna be cool!'

�֍ ✖ ✖

At another campsite nearby, Vilgax's robot was destroying everything in its path. Motorhomes and tents exploded as it unleashed power blast after power blast. It had extended to its full height, and now towered like a giant above the wreckage of the camp.

Campers ran, stumbling over each other, trying to get to safety. They screamed as yet more blasts tore the area apart. The robot wanted the Omnitrix, and it was going to find it, no matter what it had to do.

With a clanking of machinery, the android swung an arm down and grabbed one of the fleeing campers. The man screamed and kicked out, struggling to break free of the robot's clutches. It was no use though: the robot was too strong.

'Leave him alone!' boomed a voice from nearby. The robot spun round, searching for the source of the sound.

A large alien, made of what looked like green crystal, stood nearby. It was Ben in the form of the indestructible Diamondhead, and there was no way he was letting anyone get hurt.

'You want somebody to pick on?' he growled. 'Try me!'

Lights blinked behind the robot's eyes as it scanned the newcomer. It dropped the camper to the ground as its targeting system locked on to the watch. It had found the Omnitrix!

A blast of energy screeched from the robot's weapons. It slammed into the ground at Diamondhead's feet, sending the alien tumbling through the air.

With a grinding of metal, Diamondhead crashed through the roof of a motorhome. Another blast from the robot's laser turned the vehicle into a flaming heap of junk, trapping the alien inside. The giant android slowly advanced. That had been almost too easy.

It stopped in its tracks as a razor-sharp hand tore a hole in the burning metal. Diamondhead pulled himself free and studied his arm. As he watched, a dozen deadly spikes grew out from its shiny green surface.

'Cool!' he grinned, before turning his attention back to the matter at hand.

He ran forwards, swinging wildly. This form was built for strength, though not speed, and the robot easily avoided his clumsy attack. It launched itself straight up into the air, before dropping down with its spider-like legs extended.

The metal limbs knocked Diamondhead over and pinned him to the ground. He tried to move, but the robot was too heavy. He was trapped.

'Uhhh . . .' he muttered, 'I think I'm in trouble!'

A short distance away, a park ranger leaped from his car, stunned at what he was seeing.

'What's going on here?' he demanded.

Gwen shouted over her shoulder as she ran past, 'You probably wouldn't believe me if I told you!'

The ranger opened his mouth to answer, but instead screamed with fright as his car was

crushed by a falling alien. Diamondhead pulled
himself up from the wreckage and gave his
head a shake. He was dazed. If he could just
take a moment to recover, he'd –

No time! He threw himself clear, just
before a power blast turned the car into an oily
spot on the ground.

Before Diamondhead could get back
to his feet, the robot wrapped a huge, metal
claw round him and lifted him high into the
air. Another claw wrapped round his arm. He
felt a sharp pain shoot through his shoulder as
the android gave a violent tug. Diamondhead
gasped as he realised what was happening.

The robot was tearing him apart!

CHAPTER SIX

A TASTE OF THEIR OWN MEDICINE

Diamondhead gritted his teeth. The pain was almost too much to bear. If he didn't do something fast, his arm was going to be ripped clean off!

Concentrating hard, he forced shards of diamond to extend out from his trapped arm. They tore through the robot's metal claw, damaging the wiring inside. The android staggered backwards as its arm exploded.

The hand holding Diamondhead fired a piercing power blast, sending him hurtling towards a toilet block. The brick walls crumbled as he smashed through them, head first.

'Ben!' shouted Grandpa helplessly.

But Ben wasn't done for yet. He stumbled from what was left of the toilet block and approached the robot. This fight wasn't over!

He threw up his arms to protect himself as the android launched another power blast. The beam hit his shiny diamond surface and bounced off in every direction. Grandpa, Gwen and the other campers were forced to duck and dodge to avoid the spray of blasts.

Diamondhead watched the beams reflect off his body. His polished surface acted almost like a mirror. That gave him an idea!

'Come on,' he barked, pointing to his chest, 'burn one in here.'

Gwen and Grandpa couldn't believe their ears. Was Ben really inviting the robot to blast him?

'Get out of there!' Grandpa cried. 'Run!'

Diamondhead ignored him. There was no

way he was going to run. He had a plan!

The robot fired his weapon. As the energy crackled towards him, Diamondhead held up his hands. They glowed white hot under the force of the blast.

'Let's see how *you* like it, you techno freak!' he growled.

With a roar of effort, Diamondhead pushed back against the blast, deflecting its deadly beam. The laser curved wildly. It cut a trench in the rocky ground and sliced several trees in half, but with one final effort the alien

directed it towards its real target.

The beam sliced the robot neatly in two. As the top half slid to the ground, the bottom shuddered and shook. Twin explosions ripped through both broken parts, destroying them from the inside out.

'All right!' cheered Grandpa. 'Way to go, Be–' He stopped, realising all the other campers were watching him. Maybe it'd be best if they didn't know who had *really* saved the day. 'Uh . . . diamond-headed guy.'

'Oh, yeah! Who's bad?' Diamondhead laughed. He twisted his arms and shook his butt in a dance of celebration. The campers stared at him. Was this guy crazy? 'Well,' he coughed, noticing their looks, 'I think my work here is done.'

And, with that, he ran off into the woods, as fast as his indestructible legs would carry him.

❈ ❈ ❈

Floating inside his life-support tube, Vilgax was furious. He had been following events on his ship's view screen. Things had not gone according to plan.

'Failure,' he scowled. 'Unbelievable! The puny Earth-being that is keeping the Omnitrix from me will soon hang on my trophy wall!'

His red eyes grew dark and narrow. It would take time for him to heal, but heal he would. Soon he would make the boy pay. Soon he would make the whole pathetic planet pay!

He looked down at the stumps where his legs should be.

Soon, but not quite yet . . .

⊗ ⊗ ⊗

The next morning, Grandpa and Gwen were packing up The Rust Bucket and preparing to move on. Grandpa finished loading a box into the motorhome and looked around. Something was missing.

'Where's Ben?'

Gwen shrugged. 'I haven't seen him since breakfast.'

A sudden wind whipped up from nowhere and tore through the camp. Grandpa stepped back in surprise as a sleek, blue-and-black alien named XLR8 skidded to a halt right beside him.

'Ben?'

'Yup,' the alien replied. 'Hey, check this out!'

Grandpa and Gwen blinked in surprise. They'd hardly noticed the alien move, but suddenly all their belongings were stacked neatly inside The Rust Bucket.

'Pretty fast, huh?' beamed Ben in his alien form.

With a **BLEEP BLEEP BLEEP BLEEEEP!** and a blinding flash, the alien turned back into plain old Ben Tennyson.

'I think this is going to be the best summer ever,' he grinned.

'Absolutely,' nodded Grandpa Max.

'It's definitely going to be interesting,' Gwen agreed. 'So, where'd you go, anyway?'

'Just had to take care of a few things,' he smirked.

✖ ✖ ✖

Back in the playground of Ben's school, two bullies found themselves dangling from a tree by their underwear. How had they got there? Neither one of them had any idea. What they did know was that whatever it was that had happened to them had happened very, *very* fast!

✖ ✖ ✖

Ben couldn't help but chuckle as he took his seat in The Rust Bucket. That robot wasn't the only one to have been given a taste of its own medicine!

He leaned back, his hands behind his head, as Grandpa started the engine. Ben wasn't sure what adventures lay ahead, or what other surprises the watch had in store for him. He knew one thing for certain though – it was going to be a whole lot of fun finding out!

BEN 10 BOOK COLLECTION

HAVE YOU SEEN THEM ALL?

Ben 10 Alien Force Annual 2010	978 1 4052 4653 8; £7.99
Ben 10 Alien Force colour storybook 1 (Ben 10 Returns Part 1/Part 2)	978 1 4052 4799 3; £4.99
Ben 10 Alien Force colour storybook 2 (The Gauntlet/Be-Knighted)	978 1 4052 4800 6; £4.99
Ben 10 Amazing 3D Hero Vision	978 1 4052 4413 8; £3.99
Ben 10 Puzzle and Quiz Book	978 1 4052 4492 3; £3.99
Ben 10 Magnet Book	978 1 4052 4599 9; £5.99
Ben 10 All Action Stories & Flicker Book	978 1 4052 4512 8; £4.99
Ben 10 comic book 1 (And Then There Were 10)	978 1 4052 4663 7; £4.99
Ben 10 comic book 2 (Washington B.C.)	978 1 4052 4664 4; £4.99
Ben 10 comic book 3 (The Krakken)	978 1 4052 4804 4; £4.99

Ben 10 comic book 4
(Permanent Retirement)   978 1 4052 4805 1; £4.99

Ben 10 chapter storybook 1
(And Then There Were 10/Kevin 11)   978 1 4052 4467 1; £3.99

Ben 10 chapter storybook 2
(The Alliance/Secrets)   978 1 4052 4468 8; £3.99

Ben 10 chapter storybook 3
(Truth/Framed)   978 1 4052 4672 9; £4.99

Ben 10 chapter storybook 4
(The Galactic Enforcers/Ultimate Weapon) 978 1 4052 4673 6; £4.99

COMING SOON ...
3 COOL NEW BEN 10 BOOKS!

Ben 10 Alien Force Extreme (Pop-Up) 978 1 4052 4852 5; £14.99

Ben 10 Alien Force chapter storybook 1
(All That Glitters/Max Out)   978 1 4052 5006 1; £4.99

Ben 10 Alien Force chapter storybook 2
(Paradox/Plumbers' Helpers)   978 1 4052 5007 8; £4.99

Visit Egmont.co.uk